MEG'S MUMMY

by Helen Nicoll
and Jan Pieńkowski

PUFFIN BOOKS

They flew
up the Nile

and landed on a pyramid

She peered
in the door

She discovered a huge hall

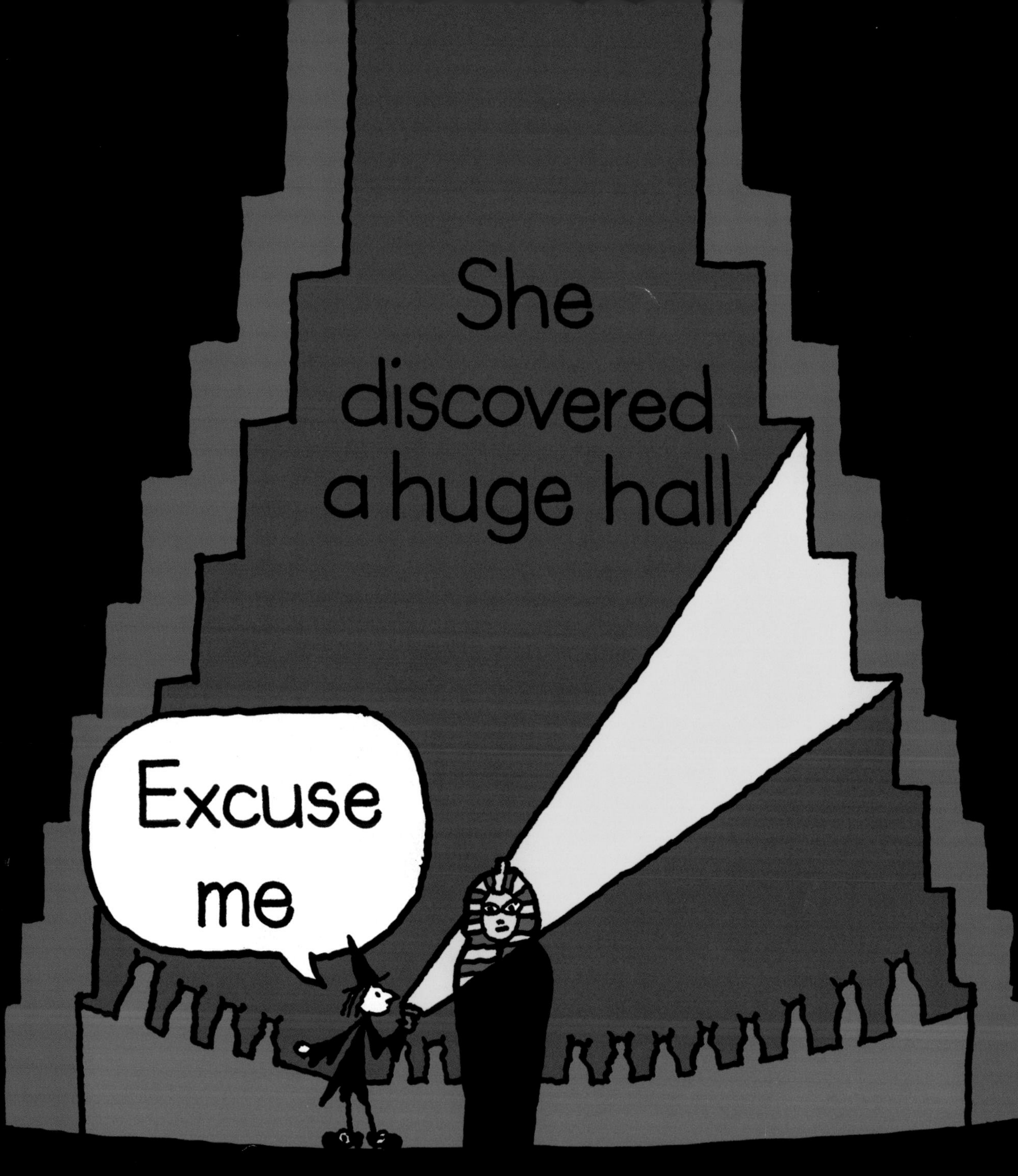

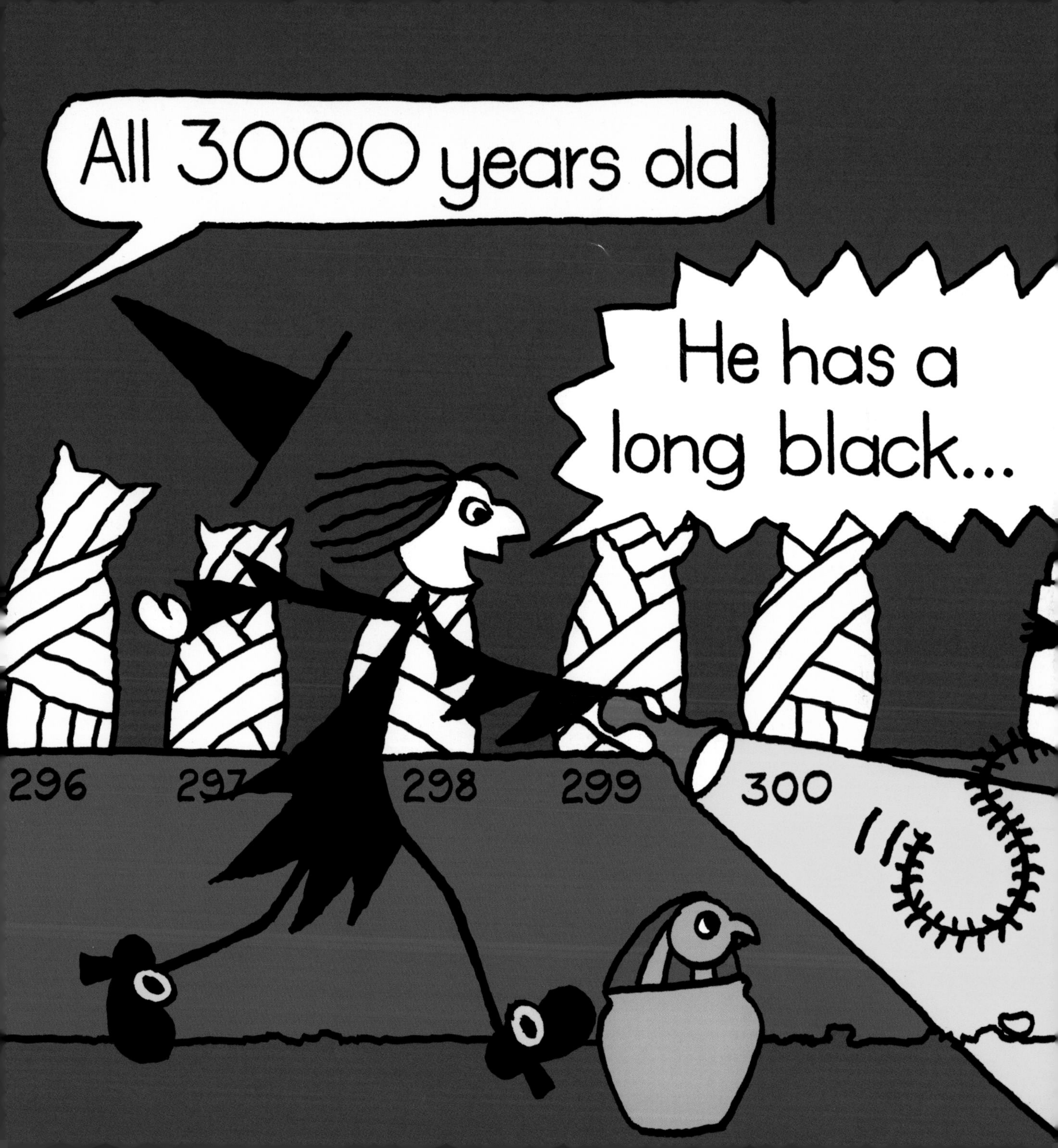
All 3000 years old
He has a long black...
296
297
298
299
300

It was a crocodile

Goodbye!

for Kuba

PUFFIN BOOKS
Published by the Penguin Group, London, New York, Australia, Canada, India, New Zealand and South Africa
Penguin Books Ltd, Registered Offices: 80 Strand, London WC2R 0RL, England
www.penguin.com
Published 2004
10 9 8 7 6 5 4 3 2 1
Text copyright © Helen Nicoll, 2004
Illustrations copyright © Jan Pieńkowski, 2004
Story and characters copyright © Helen Nicoll and Jan Pieńkowski, 2004
Lettering by Caroline Austin
Manufactured in China
British Library Cataloguing in Publication Data
A CIP catalogue record for this book is available from the British Library
ISBN 0-141-38071-3